GREEK BEASTS AND HEROES

The Sailor Snatchers

D0109636

You can read the stories in the
Greek Beasts and Heroes series in any order,
but Atticus finishes his quest in this book.

To read more about some of the characters in
this book, turn to pages 78 and 79
to find out which other books to try.

If you'd like to know where Atticus has
been so far, then read the series in order ...

GREEK BEASTS AND HEROES

The Sailor Snatchers

LUCY COATS
Illustrated by Anthony Lewis

Orion
Children's Books

Text and illustrations first appeared in
Atticus the Storyteller's 100 Greek Myths
First published in Great Britain in 2002
by Orion Children's Books
This edition published in Great Britain in 2010
by Orion Children's Books
a division of the Orion Publishing Group Ltd
Orion House
5 Upper St Martin's Lane
London WC2H 9EA
An Hachette UK company

1 3 5 7 9 8 6 4 2

A catalogue record for this book is available from the British Library

ISBN 978 1 4440 0076 4

Printed in China

www.orionbooks.co.uk
www.lucycoats.com

For all my lovely readers who have stuck
with Atticus and Melissa to the end of our
shared journey around ancient Greece.
Thank you.
L. C.

For Dad
A. L.

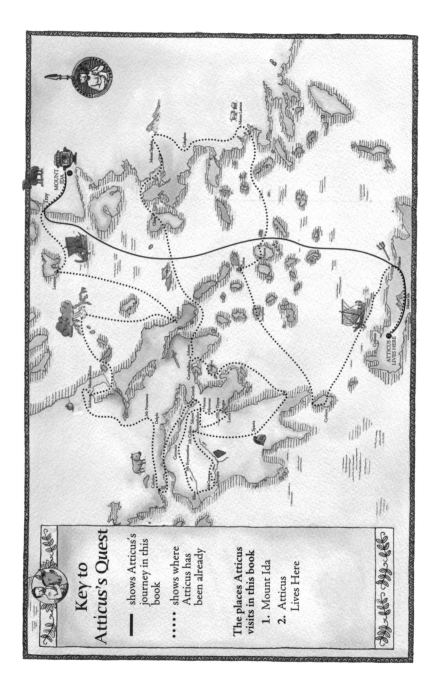

Key to
Atticus's Quest

— shows Atticus's journey in this book

····· shows where Atticus has been already

The places Atticus visits in this book

1. Mount Ida
2. Atticus Lives Here

Contents

Stories from the Heavens

L ong ago, in ancient Greece, gods and goddesses, heroes and heroines lived together with fearful monsters and every kind of fabulous beast that ever flew, or walked or swam. But little by little, as people began to build more villages and towns and cities, the gods and monsters disappeared into the secret places of the world and the heavens, so that they could have some peace.

Before they disappeared,
the gods and goddesses gave
the gift of storytelling to
men and women, so that
nobody would ever forget them. They
ordered that there should be a great
storytelling festival once every seven
years on the slopes of Mount Ida, near
Troy, and that tellers of tales should
come from all over Greece and from
lands near and far to take part. Every

 seven years a
beautiful painted vase,
filled to the brim with gold,
magically appeared as a
first prize, and the winner
was honoured for the rest of his life by all
the people of Greece.

It was the third day of the Festival and Atticus beamed delightedly. People kept coming up and congratulating him on how well he had told his Cyclops story, and now Captain Nikos and the crew had turned up.

"I hear you're the best of the bunch," roared Nikos.

"Not really," said Atticus. "And there's still a long way to go till the end of the competition."

"We'll be cheering you on," said Nikos, as Atticus walked out to tell his first story of the day.

The Enchantress and the Pigs

Aeolus, the Keeper of the Winds, waved goodbye to Odysseus's fleet as it left his island.

"Remember what I told you, Odysseus," he called. "Don't open that little bag I gave you till you are safely home!"

As the soft westerly breeze blew on, Odysseus lay back on the deck with a tired sigh and slept. As the sun rose on the second day the fleet came within sight of Ithaca. The smoke could be seen rising from the chimneys of his palace, and still he slept on.

"What do you think is in that bag?" said the sailors to one another.

"Do you think it could be gold? Or jewels? Or a magic gift? Surely it wouldn't hurt to have just one little peek. We're nearly home after all, and Odysseus is asleep, he'll never know."

So they crept up to the sleeping man and untied the strings.

As they bent over to see what was inside, there was a tremendous whooshing and swooshing noise and they were all blown backwards.

Above the ship the three fierce winds which Aeolus had trapped in the little bag fought and battled and

 13

whipped up a great storm which blew the ships apart and scattered them all over the oceans.

"What have you done?" cried Odysseus, as he woke with a jump. "Now we shall never get home!" And he buried his head in his hands and wept.

Of the twelve ships battered by that awful storm, only Odysseus' survived. It eventually came to land safely on a little wooded island covered in oaks and beeches and other tall forest trees.

Fierce-looking lions and tigers and wolves prowled on the shore, but instead of roaring and howling, they purred and whined and rolled over to have their bellies tickled.

Odysseus sent his friend Eurylochus and twenty-two men to investigate.

They followed the capering, leaping beasts into the forest, and soon they came to a higgledy-piggledy house in a clearing, with vines growing round the door.

A feast was set out on long tables, and a pretty woman with long golden hair was waiting at its head. It was Circe, the Enchantress of the Isle of Dawn.

"Come and eat!" she said. "All guests are welcome at my table!"

The twenty-two sailors rushed forward and started grabbing at the delicious food and stuffing it into their mouths.

Eurylochus was suspicious, though, and hid behind a tree.

Suddenly he saw Circe whip out a wand from behind her back and tap each sailor on the top of his head. What happened next was horrible.

A loud grunting and squealing noise came from each man's mouth, and as they got up from the table, he saw that they had all been turned into hairy pigs.

"Into the sty with you, you greedy things," said Circe. Eurylochus ran straight back to Odysseus to tell him what had happened.

 17

Odysseus seized his sword and dashed off to the rescue. But on his way he met the god Hermes.

"Not so fast, my friend," said Hermes. "You'll need this!"

And he gave Odysseus a small, white flower with a black root. "If you have this in your pocket she won't be able to enchant you," he said, grinning. "But don't tell Zeus or Poseidon that I helped you!"

Odysseus thanked the god, and soon he had reached Circe's house.

As before a delicious feast was set out, and Circe welcomed her guest with kind words.

Odysseus ate and drank thankfully – he was very hungry after the storm.

But when Circe crept up behind and tapped him with her wand, nothing happened. She stared at the wand and shook it hopefully, muttering some magic words, but still her enchantment didn't work. Then she laughed and went to the sty where she turned all the pigs back into men.

"You have beaten me, great Odysseus," she said. "You and your men must stay with me for a year while you mend your ship, and then I will help you to get home."

Odysseus agreed happily, but you may be sure that he took her wand away and made Circe promise not to do any more of her enchantments while he and his men were on her magic island.

The clapping had stopped and the crowd was buzzing expectantly. Atticus could see Captain Nikos and the crew and Callimachus sitting together in the shade. He looked at the judges. They were smiling and scribbling on their wax tablets. The last storyteller had been very good.

"Atticus of Crete!" called the judges.

Atticus strode confidently into the arena for his second turn. "The tale of Odysseus and Tiresias," he announced.

Ghosts from the Underworld

As Odysseus sailed away from the Isle of Dawn, Circe set an enchanted mist around his ship.

"Even Zeus cannot see through this," she said, "and it will protect you as long as no one on your ship sneezes three times in a row."

Circe had told Odysseus that before he could go home to Ithaca, he must first go and see Tiresias, greatest of all the Greek seers, to learn what his future would be. The only trouble was that Tiresias was dead and lived down in Tartarus.

"How on earth do I get to Tartarus?" asked Odysseus. "Surely I can't sail to the Underworld?"

But Circe nodded. "If you sail north-west into a northerly wind and follow the stream of Ocean till you come to Persephone's grove of black poplars and willows, you will find the gates of the Underworld on your left-hand side," she said, and then she told him just what to do when he got there.

Now sailing north-west into a northerly breeze is normally quite impossible, but with Circe's magical help Odysseus's ship soon landed on the shore just by Persephone's grove.

There he dug a trench, which he filled with a mixture of blood and ewe's milk, and waited with his sword drawn. Soon a whispering and a rustling sound came up from the long dark passage behind the gates, and as they creaked open a grey mass of ghosts poured through.

"Blood and milk," they hissed. "Give us blood and milk to drink!"

Odysseus held them off with his sword, until Tiresias finally arrived, and very hard work it was.

 23

The ghost of the ancient seer bent his head to drink, and then he looked at Odysseus. "Great danger and great trouble," he said. "I see the years before you and the years behind. What you have conquered so far is nothing to what you will have to face at home from the greedy men who want your wife and your kingdom. But you will win victory at the end with the help of the goddess Athene!"

"But when?" asked Odysseus. "When shall I get home and what dangers shall I face before I get there?" Tiresias was fading away, but Odysseus heard his answer, like a faint whisper in the still air.

"Long years! Long years before you see Ithaca again. Beware the singers, beware the cliffs, beware the taste of the sun god's island cattle."

Odysseus bowed and thanked him with tears in his eyes, and then he let the other ghosts drink. He saw many old friends and loved ones that day – his mother, and his old comrades Achilles and Agamemnon – even the ghost of great Heracles himself came to wish him luck. But in the evening he had to return to his ship.

"Atishoo, atishoo, atishoo!" he sneezed as the grey ghostly fog of Tartarus tickled his nose. Circe's magic mist disappeared at once, and Zeus soon saw that Odysseus's ship was sailing on the ocean again.

"Ho! Brother Poseidon!" he called. "Let's see if we can whip up a real storm this time." And the lightning flashed and the thunder roared as the two gods laughed, and Odysseus and his long-suffering crew were driven out amongst the crashing waves once more.

Atticus patted Melissa. "I'm sorry to leave you alone so much," he said. "But they don't allow donkeys to come and watch, I'm afraid."

Melissa butted him in the stomach and snuffled into his hand. She was quite happy. Callimachus cut big bunches of dry grass for her every day, and there was a nice stream nearby.

Then the trumpet sounded its single note loudly for the beginning of the fourth day . . .

"Time to go," said Callimachus. "You've got stories to tell."

The Death Singers

"**L**and ahoy!" shouted the sailor at the masthead. Odysseus ran to have a look.

What he saw made his heart sink right down into his shabby sandals. It was a little island, far off in the distance.

On the island was a group of figures. The sun was glinting off the strings of the golden instruments they carried, and a faint sound of music and singing reached his ears.

Odysseus knew he must not panic. Circe had warned him about this terrible place, and he knew just what to do. He ordered his sailors to stuff wax in their ears, and to get out the oars.

 28

"Now row as hard as you can when I give the signal," he commanded them. "Don't look to right or left, and whatever you do don't unblock your ears or we shall all die."

"But what about you, your Majesty?" asked one of his sailors. "What are you going to do?"

Odysseus grinned. "I'm going to be tied to the mast so tightly that I can't possibly escape," he said. "I'm going to be the only man ever to listen to the voices of the Sirens and live!"

The sailors tied Odysseus to the mast, and then they started to row for their lives.

The magical music of the golden harps and the singing came closer and closer, and soon Odysseus was screaming for his men to untie him so that he could swim closer to the wonderful sounds. But they could not hear him.

He turned to look at the little island. All around it lay the wrecks of a hundred ships, and on its rocky shores lay the skulls and bones of a thousand sailors, all of whom had listened to the fatal song of the Sirens and died trying to reach them.

The four Sirens themselves sat in a lovely meadow of bright summer flowers. They had the faces of beautiful women, but their bodies were covered in shimmering feathers which glittered and glimmered in the sunlight with all the colours of the rainbow.

"Come to us!" they sang in high sweet voices. "Come to us, Odysseus, bravest of brave heroes! We will tell you the future!"

Odysseus shouted and threatened his crew, but it was no good, the ropes around him held fast, and soon the island was far behind them, and the spell of the Sirens' song was broken for ever.

Odysseus's men untied him and unplugged their ears. "Now perhaps we shall have a bit of peace," they muttered, as they hoisted the sails once again for home.

But unfortunately Zeus had another terrible treat in store for them.

The smoke of hundreds of midday cooking fires drifted into the still air, and the cries of the food-sellers rose above the yatter and chatter of the crowds. More and more people were pouring in to listen to the storytellers, and in corners behind stalls and tents bets were being taken.

"25-1 on Atticus of Crete to get to day five," hissed a quiet voice as Atticus passed. Atticus smiled. He didn't think he had much hope of getting through to the top ten, but you never knew. He turned into the arena and sat down in a shady corner.

There was just time for a nap before he was called to perform.

The Sailor Snatchers

Not many weeks after they had escaped from the Sirens, Odysseus and his men came to an even greater danger, and this time there was no escape.

To get home to Ithaca they had to sail through a narrow rocky passage with high cliffs on either side.

On one side of the cliffs, high up in a cave, lived the dreadful monster, Scylla, who had six bright green heads, each on a long snaky neck. Each head had a set of snapping razor teeth, and every time a ship sailed past Scylla would reach down and snatch a sailor in each of her six mouths.

Then she would crunch and chew the poor men until their bones cracked and their blood dripped into the sea below.

Deep down in the sea at the other side of the passage lived another terrible monster called Charybdis, a fat bubble-like thing, with a huge mouth and blubbery lips. She sat at the bottom of the ocean, sucking and blowing, blowing and sucking, until the water above swirled into spouts and whisked into whirlpools so big that no ship could survive being caught in them.

Circe had warned Odysseus about these monsters too. "You will have to go through them," she said. "But whatever you do, don't go near Charybdis, who lives on the right. You may lose some men to Scylla, but at least you will survive. If you get caught by Charybdis, you will all die."

So Odysseus thought up a crafty plan. He told his men about the danger of the water-sucking monster, but he didn't say anything about the one in the cliff above.

"If I tell them about Scylla," he thought, "they'll be too afraid to go through at all."

As the helmsman steered carefully past the dreadful Charybdis, there was a whistling sound.

Six sailors were snatched into mid-air, and as their horrified companions watched, they were gobbled up in a minute.

"Row! Row for your lives!" roared Odysseus, seizing an oar.

And row they did. Soon they had landed far away on a lovely green island where shining black and white and red cattle grazed among the long juicy grass.

"A feast!" cried the men. "Let us have a feast!" But Odysseus remembered Tiresias's warning, and ordered them not to touch the cows.

"We still have some of the provisions Circe gave us," he said. "Let us eat those instead. We shall offend the sun god himself if we eat these cattle, and Zeus knows we can't afford to do that!"

But soon another storm rose up, preventing them from leaving the island,

and after weeks and weeks of rain and wind all the food was gone.

The men got so hungry that Odysseus could not stop them killing and cooking one small cow, although he himself refused to touch a bite.

As soon as the last mouthful had been eaten, the storm dropped and the sun came out. Odysseus and his men hurried to their ship and cast off.

"See!" said the sailors. "It didn't do any harm."

 39

Just at that moment Helios the sun god noticed that one of his precious cows was missing. He gave a great roar of anger, and the storm came back stronger than ever.

Helios was so angry that he got Zeus to throw a thunderbolt at the ship, which split it in half. All the sailors drowned except Odysseus, who clung on to the mast and keel, which he tied together to make a raft.

By the morning he was being blown back towards Scylla and Charybdis, and even crafty Odysseus was in despair.

But just above the whirlpool grew
a little fig tree, and as Charybdis
sucked down the mast
and keel, Odysseus made a
great leap and clung to it
until the bits of wood
appeared again.

He dropped down on them and floated away to safety. His bravery and spirit were so great that Zeus finally took pity on him and hid him from the monsters' eyes.

Exhausted, he lay there and let the winds and waves blow him where they wanted.

For nine days and nine nights he rocked and drifted on the cradle of the ocean. And on the tenth day he was washed through a magical mist and onto the shores of the Island of Ogygia, which, although he didn't know it then, was where he would spend the next seven years of his life.

Nine names had been read out so far, and Atticus was not among them. The judge cleared his throat.

"And the last successful competitor is . . . Atticus of Crete." There was a storm of clapping and cheering. Atticus felt quite faint and had to be held up by Callimachus and Captain Nikos. He had got through to the fifth day!

The judge shook Atticus by the hand. "Well done!" he said. "Now you have to choose the two stories you will tell today".

"Odysseus has brought me luck so far," said Atticus. "I'll tell the stories of Calypso and Nausicaa."

"A good choice," said the judge.

The Island of Mists

O dysseus stared out through the magical mist that prevented him leaving the Island of Ogygia, tears running down his cheeks as they had done every day for the last seven years.

Although the beautiful nymph, Calypso, who ruled the island, had given him his every desire, Odysseus was unhappy. What use were jewelled swords, and baths of asses' milk, and armour as light as silk and endless endless parties when all he wanted was to go home to his wife Penelope and his son, Telemachus.

"He must be a man by now," wept Odysseus. "And I haven't been there to teach him any of the things a father should. Someone else will have taught him to use a sword, and to ride a horse, and to plough a field. Someone else will have taught him to sail a ship and to throw a spear."

Then he prayed to the goddess Athene to help him.

Athene was very fond of Odysseus, but she had not dared to go against her father Zeus and her uncle Poseidon.

However, Poseidon was away from Olympus and Athene begged Zeus to allow the wandering hero to return home at last.

"Please, father," she said, fluttering her long silver eyelashes. "You know how you admire his bravery."

 45

So Zeus commanded Hermes to fly down to Calypso and order her to let Odysseus go.

Calypso cried and cried, because she really did love Odysseus, but she had to obey Zeus.

"I shall even help him to build a raft," she sniffed as she went to find Odysseus and tell him the good news.

Odysseus whistled and sang as he chopped down trees for the raft. Calypso and her maidens sat sadly beside him as they wove strong ropes to lash it together.

Finally it was ready. Calypso loaded it with provisions and gave Odysseus many presents, including a wonderful embroidered robe she had made herself.

 46

The silken sail was raised, and the raft moved slowly out to sea.

"Remember me," cried Calypso as she waved goodbye to the man she loved. And Odysseus raised his hand in farewell as the curtains of mist opened in front of him and he sailed out onto the ocean once more.

"Bad luck," said the competitor who had just sat down next to Atticus.

"What?" said Atticus, waking up with a start. "What do you mean?"

"The lists have just gone up for this afternoon," said the man, laughing unpleasantly. "And you're going right at the end. The judges will be bored by then."

"My old mother always told me that the best comes last," said Atticus. The man grunted and spat as he moved away.

"He's just jealous that I chose such good stories," Atticus said to Callimachus.

But as the long hot afternoon drew on and the judges drooped and snored, he wasn't so sure.

The Golden Ball

Poseidon waved away Iris the messenger as he peered at the magic map of his ocean kingdom which lay spread out before him.

"I'm busy," he said, frowning fiercely as she tried to hand him Zeus's letter telling him that Odysseus was now free to go home.

While he watched, he noticed a small speck setting off from Calypso's island. As it grew bigger, he saw that it was a man on a raft – a man he knew and hated.

"Wretched Odysseus!" he roared, and he swirled his trident so hard that the waves rose up as high as houses.

The raft was flung into the air, and all the precious gifts that Calypso had given Odysseus sank to the bottom of the sea. Odysseus himself was thrown into the cold rough water. His embroidered robes became so heavy and soggy that they started to drag him down as he struggled to stay afloat.

"Athene!" he gurgled as he fought to get out of his clothes. "Help me!"

As he spoke, a seagull flew over and dropped a silken veil on the water.

 50

"Tie that around you," she screeched. "It will save you from drowning!"

Odysseus tied the veil around his waist and began to swim.

He swam and swam and swam until he was exhausted. But the magical veil held him up above the waves and at last he floated to the shores of another island. He crawled into a grove of trees by a little stream, pulled some dry leaves over him, and fell into a deep sleep.

He was woken by giggles and peals of laughter. Sitting up, he saw a group of girls playing with a golden ball, while others washed clothes in the stream.

Suddenly, the ball bounced and came to rest just by his feet. The tallest girl ran after it and when she saw Odysseus she let out a little scream.

"Don't be afraid," said Odysseus. "I am Odysseus of Ithaca. If you will take me to the king of this place, I will explain everything."

The girl, whose name was Nausicaa, happened to be King Alcinous's daughter. She gave Odysseus some clothes, and took him up to the palace, where her father was delighted to receive such a famous hero.

"Welcome to Phaecia! We all thought you were dead long ago," he said, and after giving Odysseus a magnificent feast, King Alcinous gave him many rich gifts to replace those he had lost, as well as a crew and a boat to take him back to Ithaca.

Odysseus fell asleep on the voyage home, and so the king's sailors carried him gently off the boat and laid him down on the shores of his own land at long last, stacking his gifts at his feet.

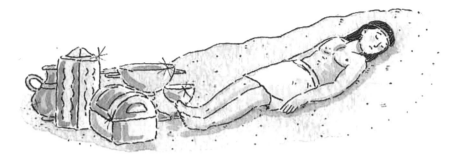

Now Poseidon was so angry with King Alcinous for helping Odysseus that he turned the king's ship and all its sailors to stone on their voyage home to Phaecia. King Alcinous had to sacrifice twelve of his best bulls to Poseidon to stop him dropping a great stone mountain on the harbour.

"That's the very last time I help some handsome hero you've picked up off the beach," he said crossly to Nausicaa. But Nausicaa just smiled.

The last five had just been announced.

Atticus had got through!

The crowd surged around him and his four fellow storytellers, patting backs and shouting, while the judges waved their hands and called for quiet. Finally, one of them seized a great brass gong and beat it till silence fell. He held out a leather bag filled with silver discs.

"Atticus of Crete will pick a story first," he said.

Atticus stepped forward and stuck his hand into the bag. The discs felt cold – all except one.

"This one," he said, pulling it out and looking at it. "The Return of Odysseus," he read out loud.

The Return of the Wanderer

When Odysseus woke up, he didn't know where he was at all.

"What is this place?" he asked sleepily as he stretched and yawned. There was a handsome shepherd boy leaning against a nearby tree.

The shepherd boy laughed, and as he did so he changed into a tall, beautiful woman wearing silver armour and a winged helmet.

"Don't you recognise your own kingdom?" said Athene. "Shame on you, Odysseus!" Odysseus looked around him and soon he saw that the goddess was right.

 56

He was home at last! He knelt down and kissed the ground as he wept with relief.

"No time for that," said Athene sternly. "Now that you are here, there is a lot of work to do. All the young men around are trying to marry your wife because they think you are dead, and your poor son is trying to protect her as well as your wine and food, which they are drinking and eating by the bucketful." Odysseus looked around wildly for his sword, but Athene stopped him.

"You will just get yourself killed if you do that," she said, shaking him.

"I have a better plan." After she had helped Odysseus to hide the treasure and gifts which King Alcinous had given him, she disguised him as an old beggar man and sent him off to find his old swineherd, Eumaeus, warning him to tell no one who he really was.

"Wait for me at Eumaeus's hut, and I shall bring someone you will want to meet," she said with a little smile.

Eumaeus was a kind old man, and when he saw the wretched beggar at his gates he asked him in and gave him food and wine from his own meagre store.

"Perhaps the gods will look more kindly on me if I share what I have with a stranger," he said sadly. "I don't think things can get much worse than they already are around here."

As Odysseus huddled unnoticed in a corner, munching some cheese, a young man strode in.

"Master Telemachus," cried Eumaeus with a shout of joy. Odysseus looked at

the son he had not seen for twenty years, and his eyes filled with tears of pride.

Telemachus was tall and strong and handsome – everything a prince of Ithaca should be. Eumaeus went out to shut up his pigs for the night, and as soon as he had left a shining mist appeared in the room and Athene stepped out.

She took a surprised Telemachus by the hand and led him over to the dark corner, where Odysseus was sitting quietly. As she lifted the beggar's disguise, Telemachus saw a tall man standing before him. The man was built like a hero, and he was smiling.

"Father?" said Telemachus in a whisper.

"My son!" said Odysseus, holding out his arms. After much hugging and weeping, Athene led them both out of the hut.

"We must keep your father's return
a secret," she said to Telemachus.

"No one must know, not even
Eumaeus or your mother. I shall disguise

your father as a beggar again and take
him to the palace. There he can see
what kind of men are courting Penelope,
and we shall make a plan to get rid of
them."

As the beggar Odysseus entered his
courtyard an old hound lifted his head
and wagged his tail.

Odysseus brushed away a tear as he
recognised his best hunting dog, Argus.
"At least my dog greets me properly," he
muttered sadly to himself. "This is not
the homecoming I had planned at all."

Odysseus soon saw the sort of greedy, rude and unpleasant men who were infesting his palace like rats. Although it was the custom to treat beggars kindly, they kicked him and threw him out onto the dungheap, jeering and laughing at his rags.

"Find yourself another spot, old greybeard," they shouted as they returned to feasting on the best of Odysseus's wine and foods.

"Just you wait," growled Odysseus, rubbing his bruised shoulder. "Just you wait."

The crowd strained forward to listen. It was so quiet in the great arena that even the judge's small cough sounded like one of Zeus' thunderclaps.

"The three Golden Storytellers of the Thirty-Ninth Mount Ida storytelling festival are as follows."

The silence grew even deeper.

"Timon of Byzantium."

The crowd cheered as a dark, curly-haired man with a wide grin stepped forward waving.

"Corinna of Eleusis."

The cheers grew even more wild as a tiny woman with wrinkled apple cheeks hobbled into the arena, blowing kisses to the crowd.

Atticus dug his nails into his damp palms. It was now or never.

"Atticus of Crete."

The crowd erupted. Atticus found himself being carried shoulder high towards the arena through the shouting, laughing throng. He raised his fists in triumph. He was actually in the final of the greatest storytelling competition in the world, and what's more he knew exactly which story he was going to tell.

The End of the Journey

Penelope sat in her bedchamber staring at the wonderful tapestry she had made. For many long years she had held her suitors off by promising that she would marry one of them when it was finished. Each day she had stitched and stitched, but each night she had unpicked most of what she had done to buy just a

little more time. Now her trick had been discovered and tomorrow she would have to choose one of the suitors, and the day after that she would have to marry him.

"Oh Odysseus, my love," she sighed. "Where are you? Why don't you come home?"

And a single tear ran down her lovely cheek and dropped onto her hand, where it shone like a diamond.

At that moment there was a knock at the door. It was the old nurse, Eurycleia.

"Beg pardon, my lady," she said. "But there's an old beggar man asking to see you. He says he has news of Odysseus."

Penelope jumped up. "Bring him in at once," she cried.

While Eurycleia bustled round making the old man comfortable, Penelope listened to his story.

"Odysseus will soon be back in Ithaca," said the old beggar.

Penelope sighed. "But how am I to hold off the suitors?" she asked. "I have promised them an answer tomorrow." The old beggar scratched his head.

"Do you still have Odysseus's great bow? The one only he could draw?" Penelope nodded. "Then tell the suitors that whoever can draw the bow and shoot it through twelve axe-rings shall be your next husband." Just then Eurycleia gave a gasp. As she was washing the beggar's feet she noticed a great white scar on his ankle. Only one person had a scar like that!

"Odyss . . ." she started, but Athene clapped an invisible hand over her mouth so she couldn't speak. Odysseus shook his head at her and put his finger to his lips.

The next day, before the usual feast began, Telemachus escorted Penelope down to the hall to speak to the suitors. She held up the great bow and told them what she wanted them to do. Meanwhile Eumaeus bustled about, setting up the axe-heads in a straight row. Each suitor in turn took up the great bow and wrestled with it. Some managed to string it, some even managed to fit an arrow on the string, but none could pull it.

"Is there not one man in this hall who is as good as my husband, Odysseus?" cried Penelope scornfully. Then the old beggar who had been sitting in the corner stepped forward.

"I will try," he said. All the suitors laughed and jeered, and several of them even stepped forward to throw him out again. But Penelope held up her hand.

"Let him try!" she ordered. The beggar stripped off his ragged cloak and the suitors all gasped suddenly at the size of his muscles. He picked up the bow and stroked it. Then he strung it, fixed an arrow to the string and pulled it back to his ear in one swift smooth motion. The arrow whistled as it left the bow and swooshed through every one of the axe-rings. Suddenly a golden mist surrounded the beggar man, and his disguise fell away.

"I am Odysseus!" he cried to the astonished suitors. "And you are no longer welcome in my hall!" The suitors rushed to the walls to pull down the spears that had been hanging there, but

Telemachus had taken them away the day before. As Eumaeus locked the doors, Telemachus and Odysseus ran towards the suitors and started killing them, while a terrified Penelope ran to her room and locked herself in.

It was a long and bloody battle, but at last all the suitors lay dead on the floor.

Athene took all the bodies away with a magical sweep of her hand.

Soon the hall was clean and sparkling once more. Penelope's door opened a crack and she peeped out into the silence. What she saw made her heart sing with joy. There were her beloved husband and son waiting for her below. A shaft of sunlight turned their robes to pure gold as she flew down the stairs with her arms held wide open.

"Welcome home, my love," she cried softly. "Welcome home at last."

Atticus Comes Home

The judges were taking a long time to
decide who had come first. A fat black
and gold vase, beautifully painted, stood
on the table in front of them. At last the
herald stepped forward to blow a fanfare
on his trumpet, and a hush fell.

"We have a winner!" boomed the chief
judge. "The gods have chosen . . ." he
paused dramatically. "Atticus of Crete!"

Captain Nikos and Callimachus and
the crowd wept and howled and cheered
and danced, while far away on the edge of

the camp a small grey donkey brayed with joy as her master was crowned with the golden laurels of the greatest storyteller in the world.

Atticus and Melissa stopped on the dusty track and looked down at the village. It lay in the late summer sunlight, the little white buildings shining like pearls. Atticus sighed. The journey home had seemed very quick. After they had put Callimachus on the boat back to Cyrene, Captain Nikos had insisted on taking them all the way to Crete, and the winds had been mild and fair all the way into the harbour at Miletus.

"Do you think they're expecting us so soon?" Atticus said to Melissa.

Melissa looked at him through her long eyelashes and then she began to trot. Faster and faster she went with Atticus running beside her. There was the shrine to Athene, there was the oil-seller's house, and there was . . . home! A row of figures was standing in the golden sunshine, looking at a cow, a pig, a cockerel and several hens. Atticus stopped in the gateway and held his arms wide, wide, wider, and the figures began to run towards him, shrieking and crying with joy.

"I'm back," he said as he disappeared in a sea of kisses and hugs and a clamour of questions. "I'm back, and I've got something to show you." Atticus went towards Melissa's saddlebags and took out two things. One was a wreath of golden laurels, and the other was a fat black and gold vase full of golden coins. He held them out to his clamouring family, who had fallen silent at last.

"Look!" said Atticus the Storyteller. "I won!"

Greek Beasts and Heroes and where to find them ...

Could you have resisted opening Odysseus's mysterious bag to find out what was inside? Pandora had a similar problem with curiosity. Find out what happened in *The Beasts in the Jar* in the story of that title.

Would you like to find out how Persephone came to spend so much time in the Underworld? Her story is in "The Queen of the Underworld" in *The Magic Head*.  That story also mentions Helios, one of the most important gods of all. You can read about him in "The Runaway Sun" in *The Dolphin's Message*.

Nymphs were pretty nature spirits, and there are lots in Atticus's stories. Thetis was a caring nymph, who rescued Hephaestus and looked after him for nine years. (See "The Lame Blacksmith" for that story.) She also had a hero son – Achilles – who you'll meet in *The Hero's Spear*. Hermes and Perseus needed the help of the Nymphs of the North in "The Snake-haired Gorgon" – read the story in *The Magic Head* to find out why it was so difficult to find out where those particular nymphs lived.

What with all those storms and waves Poseidon sent after Odysseus, it was pretty obvious he didn't like the cunning hero much, did he? You can find out how the god came to rule the sea in "The Three Gifts" which is in the very first **Greek Beasts and Heroes** volume.